That Pup!

By Lindsay Barrett George

GREENWILLOW BOOKS

An Imprint of HarperCollinsPublishers

For Susan Jaffer

That Pup!
Copyright © 2011 by Lindsay Barrett George
All rights reserved. Manufactured in China. For information address HarperCollins Children's Books,
a division of HarperCollins Publishers, 10 East 53rd Street, New York, NY 10022. www.harpercollinschildrens.com

Gouache was used to prepare the full-color art. The text type is Gill Sans Book.

Library of Congress Cataloging-in-Publication Data
George, Lindsay Barrett. That pup! / by Lindsay Barrett George. p. cm. "Greenwillow Books."
Summary: After having fun digging up acorns, a little dog decides to bury them all again.
ISBN 978-0-06-200413-0 (trade bdg.) [1. Dogs—Fiction. 2. Squirrels—Fiction. 3. Acorns—Fiction.] I. Title.
PZ7.G29334Th 2011 [E]—dc22 2010012641
11 12 13 14 15 SCP 10 9 8 7 6 5 4 3 2 1

First Edition   Greenwillow Books

One day,
my little dog
followed her nose . . .

and stopped.

She started to dig . . .

and she found an acorn.

"This is fun!" she said.
So she followed
her nose a little farther . . .

and started to dig a little more.

And she found another acorn!

Soon my little dog was finding acorns all over our yard.

She found one in a pile of leaves

and one under the wheelbarrow

and one in the pumpkin patch,

one on my car,

one among the sunflowers,

and one inside
an apple tree.

She found one on top of a stump

and one on the other side
of the pond.

Pretty soon, she had ten acorns!

My little dog
followed her nose again
and . . .

bumped into

a squirrel.

"*What are you doing?*"
asked the squirrel.

"I'm playing a game.
It's called Find the Acorn,"
said my little dog.

"Little dog," said the squirrel, "I hid those acorns. I was storing them for winter."

My little dog had an idea.

"We can play
a new game,"
she said.
"It's called Put Back the Acorn."

And so my little dog and the squirrel ran around the yard together

hiding acorns . . .

one by one.